Izzy Gizmo

and the Invention Convention

Pip Jones and Sara Ogilvie

SIMON & SCHUSTER

London   New York   Sydney   Toronto   New Delhi

IZZY GIZMO and Fixer were making a racket
(inventing a So-Sew to fix Grandpa's jacket), when

DING
DANG
DONG
DOINK!

went the bell on the door,
and a golden note fluttered down onto the floor.

From the desk of mick marvel
General secretary · Genius Guild

Ms Gizmo,
We've heard you're a whizz with invention,
so you MUST come to our annual convention!
Arrive Thursday at noon.
I do hope you're free.

Sincerely, Mick Marvel. (Please RSVP.)

Izzy gasped (as the So-Sew started to jerk).
"Me?! My machines . . . um . . . they don't always work!"

"Cobblers!" said Grandpa.

So, the very next day,
Izzy packed up her tools and they went on their way.

Over fields . . . hills . . . and waves,

they went mile after mile,

with a map that described how to reach . . .

Technoff Isle!

"Welcome, Inventors! Now, meet The Professor.
She wants you to make a machine to impress her.

If you come **first** with the thing that you build,

we'll give you a badge to the Genius Guild!

Izzy Gizmo?

Will Digg?

Maximilian Spout?

Please reply 'here!' when your name is called out.

Abi von Lavish?

And Gillian Din?

PARP!

Everyone's here!
Very good. Let's BEGIN."

Abi von Lavish's bench was pristine.
She was already building a shiny machine.

"This thing's going to make
heaps of **sparkling** jewels!
Oh dear! Tell me Izzy,
are those things your . . .

tools?!"

"Come on, Fixer!" said Izzy. "This couldn't be finer.
It'll soon be a robotic fashion designer!

It'll be SO impressive: The Magnifi-Style!
But we need some supplies, I'll be back in a while!"

Izzy dashed to the Cog Store!

But to her despair . . .

Abi von Lavish was already there.

Izzy rushed to the Wire Shed and looked on the shelf
but Abi said, "Sorry, I need these myself."

Fixer flew off to fetch fan belts and wheels.
"Too late!" Abi smirked as she turned on her heels.

"I **must** get to work on my awesome design.
By this time tomorrow, **THAT BADGE WILL BE MINE!**"

"What NOW?" Izzy groaned. "What else can we make?
A big Bake-O-Copter for delivering cake?
A Night-Time-Erizer for turning off lights?
An Automa-Stretchy for pulling up tights?!"

"Oh, Izzy!" smiled Grandpa. "**Great** inventors produce machines which can really be put to good use."

"You're right," Izzy sighed.

From behind came a **CLUNK**!

"My drill's bust!" called Abi.

"Take it out with the junk . . ."

"Are all these tools **broken**?" Izzy gawped in dismay.

"You could mend them!
You don't have to throw them away."

Suddenly . . .

PING! Izzy had an idea.

"Quick, Fixer!" she cried.
"Bring those tools over here!

We'll make an invention to fix up this lot!
We might not have much, but we'll use what we've got."

They both worked like crazy, all through the night,
and finally finished the thing at first light.

"I do hope it works, it was quite problematic.

Presenting the
Tool-Fix-Recycle-O-Matic!

Let's test it," said Izzy.

She flicked the **'ON'** switch.

But, **oh dear!**

The contraption did nothing but twitch.

"**ARGH!** I've been wiring these plugs for an hour, but Abi von Lavish has sapped all the power.

And now look! That thingummyjig's on the blink. We have to do something.

Come ON, Fixer, think!"

Fixer flew to the door, gave his wings a good flap,
and knocked on the glass with his beak,

TIPPY-TAP!

Izzy got mad. "Fixer, **why aren't you helping?**

There's so much to fix,
you're just **cawing** and **yelping!**

FINE, go and play. You're no **use!**" Izzy cried.
She opened the door . . . and sent Fixer outside.

"Izzy," said Grandpa, "yes, you have things to mend,
and you need to find power, but where is your friend?

Are you **certain** that Fixer just wanted to play?
Go and look! You might see what he wanted to say."

Izzy watched, and remembered, feeling quite proud,
how she'd made Fixer's wings when he fell from a cloud.

He was soaring and splashing, just like a bird should.

Well, suddenly . . .

FINALLY, she . . .

UNDERSTOOD!

"Oh, Fixer! I'm sorry! **We can DO it!** We must!

There are just a few things that we need to adjust."

They used a glass dome!

And some paddles

and pipes!

And planks, pins and panels of various types . . .

"It's noon!" said Mick Marvel. "You know what that means. Inventors! It's time to **start up your machines!**"

Ignoring the thump of her heart in her chest, Izzy pressed START . . . and then hoped for the best.

As Will's Opti-Logger was starting to wheeze,

Izzy and Fixer were harnessing breeze!

While fuses were blowing on Abi's Gem-Master,
Fixer tip-tapped to make the wheel faster.

While Gillian's drums
all fell off, one by one,

Izzy's machine was being
powered by sun!

And while Mick consoled
Maximilian Spout,

Izzy cheered as the shiny,
fixed tools all popped out!

TOOT! TOOT!

"You've won first prize, Izzy!" the Professor declared.

"Oh, just **look** at all of these tools you've repaired!

Such a useful machine, and so well thought through,
deserves not just **one** badge,

but certainly . . . **TWO!**"

SIMON & SCHUSTER
First published in Great Britain in 2019 by Simon and Schuster UK Ltd
1st Floor, 222 Gray's Inn Road, London, WC1X 8HB • A CBS Company • Text copyright
© 2019 Pip Jones • Illustrations copyright © 2019 Sara Ogilvie • The right of Pip Jones
and Sara Ogilvie to be identified as the author and illustrator of this work has been
asserted by them in accordance with the Copyright, Designs and Patents Act, 1988
All rights reserved, including the right of reproduction in whole or in part in any form
A CIP catalogue record for this book is available from the British Library upon request
978-1-4711-4523-0 (HB) • 978-1-4711-4524-7 (PB) • 978-1-4711-4525-4 (eBook)
Printed in Italy • 10 9 8 7 6 5 4 3 2 1

For Mia Luna, and in memory of
your sparkling Daddy, Tristan. x - PJ

For Erika - SO